For Carlos, With Love
J.E.T

For Kaleb and Ronan
H.T.

# Duck Duck Moose

by
Judith E. Torres

illustrated by
Heather Theurer

"Can I play?" Moose asked.

"Sure," said Rabbit. Moose waited for
the jump rope to come down...

Moose tried to sit on a swing...

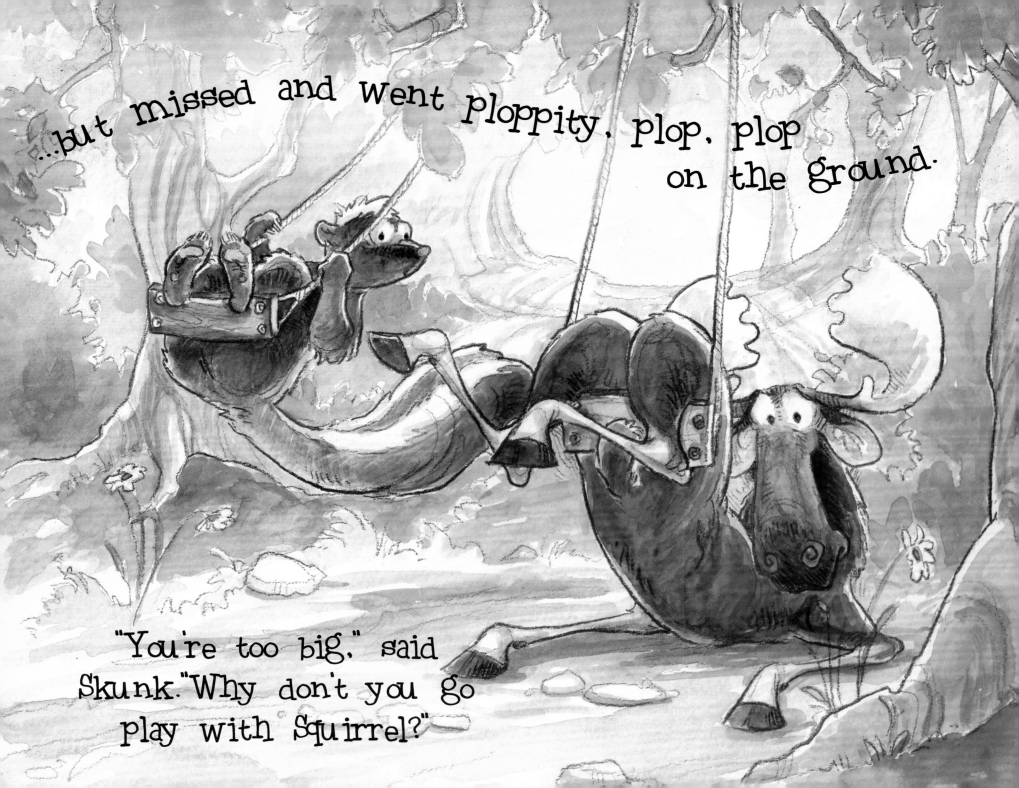

"I want to play," Moose said as he pushed his head and hooves through the monkey bars.

"I think you better go play ball
with Beaver." Raccoon panted.

"Step on up," Beaver said.
"Really?"

"Sure. When the ball comes to you, slap it as hard as you can with your tail."

Beaver threw the ball. Moose turned tail and...

Just then Eagle swooped overhead and slam dunked a
basketball into the hoop. "Want to try?"
"Do I ever!" Moose kicked the ball with his hoof and...

"Hey Moose, want to play with us?" Duck called.

"Well, you won't know until you try, will you Moose?
Come sit down and watch me." Duck directed.

"Duck, duck, duck, duck, duck, duck...

...Moose!" Duck squawked. "Try to catch me Moose!"

Moose went clickity, click, click and clompity, clomp, clomp and chased after Duck.

All the other
ducks cheered.
Duck sat down
out of breath,
"Your turn, Moose."

"Duck, duck, Moose!" Moose nudged a duck with his snout.

The duck waddled around
the circle as fast as she could, chasing after Moose.

Moose found the opening in the circle and sat...

...smiling from antler to antler.